A Follett JUST Beginning-To-Read Book

THE SNOW BABY

The Snow Baby

Margaret Hillert

Illustrated by LIZ DAUBER

FOLLETT PUBLISHING COMPANY
CHICAGO

ISBN 0-695-48146-0 Titan binding
ISBN 0-695-88146-9 Trade binding

Library of Congress Catalog Card Number: 69-15969

1011121314/807978

Come here.

Oh, come here.

See it snow.

Down, down, down it comes.

Snow, snow, snow.

See it snow.

We want to play in it.

It is fun to play in.

6

Oh, oh.

I can not find something.

Something red is not here.

Where is it?

I can not play.

8

Oh, I see it.

Here it is.

My red one is here.

I can play in the snow.

9

Look, look.

Little ones and big ones.

See the snow come down.

Run, run, run.

11

We can make snowballs.

Big, big snowballs.

Work, work, work.

12

Oh, oh.

I want one to go up here.

I can not make it go.

13

Here, here.

It is too big for you.

I can help you.

We two can make it go up.

14

Here is a little one.
It can go up here.
We can make something funny.
It is big and funny.

We can make a snow house, too.

Work, work.

Make a big house.

16

See me.

See me.

It is fun up here.

Come up, up, up.

One, two, three—jump.

We can jump into the snow.

Find me.

Find me.

18

Oh, my.
You look funny.
I look funny.
It is fun to play in the snow.

Oh, look.

Here is something.

The big one is me.

The little one is you.

And look here.

I see little spots.

One, two, three.

Three little spots in the snow.

Come, come.
We want to see where
the little spots go.
Look here, look here.

I see something.

It is little.

Is it a little snowball?

Oh, it is a baby.

A little snow baby.

Where is the mother?

Can you find the mother?

The mother is not here.

Come, little baby.

Come to me.

You can come to my house.

Away we go.

Mother, Mother.

Here is a little baby.

It can not run in the snow.

It is too little.

It can come into the house.
It can run and play in here.
We want it.
We want the snow baby.

Follett JUST Beginning-To-Read Books

Uses of these books. These books are planned for the very youngest readers, those who have been learning to read for about six to eight weeks and who have a small preprimer reading vocabulary. The books are written by Margaret Hillert, a first-grade teacher in the Royal Oak, Michigan, schools. Each book is illustrated in full color.

Children will have a feeling of accomplishment in their first reading experiences with these delightful books that they can read.

THE SNOW BABY

A charming story of a special "snow baby" and how he is found by a boy and his sister, told in 50 preprimer words.

WORD LIST

5	come (s)		find	14	too
	here		something		for
	oh		red		you
	see		where		help
	it	9	my		two
	snow		one (s)	15	a
	down		the		funny
6	we	11	look	16	house
	want		little	17	me
	to		and	18	three
	play		big		jump
	in		run		into
	is	12	make	21	spots
	fun		snowball (s)	25	baby
7	I		work		mother
	can	13	go	26	away
	not		up		